THE CHRISTMAS

TREE *express*

a novel by Allen Johnson, Jr.

Printed in the United States of America

ISBN 1-878561-21-9

Published by
Seacoast Publishing Inc.
110 12th Street North
Birmingham, Alabama 35203

for Colby and April

1

*S*PRING HAD COME SLOWLY TO MASONVILLE, Vermont, but on the fourth day of June 1937, the tiny village nestled in the foothills of the Green Mountains was bursting with new life. Birds nesting in the maple trees and elms outside the Flint farmhouse had been singing their heads off. Better than an alarm clock, they had woken Betsy Flint who, after a long satisfying stretch and a moment of reflection on a farm wife's endless cycle of work, put on a robe and went down to start breakfast. She was a pretty, plump woman with brown hair pulled back in a practical ponytail. As she stirred up the coals in the wood-burning cook-stove, she smiled knowing that the smell of bacon frying would have the usual effect of waking her husband, John, and her son, TJ. Soon, the wonderful smell found its way upstairs.

TJ woke with a pleasant feeling of invulnerability. He'd been dreaming he was on the end of a dock with a bear between him and the land, but somehow he'd known he was dreaming. As the bear approached, he'd waited calmly 'til the last moment to wake himself out of the predicament. He lay snug in his little bedroom under the eaves of the old stone house listening to his mother bustle around the kitchen, and the smell of bacon frying made his mouth water. Suddenly, he remembered the O'Conner twins and, just as suddenly, TJ lost his appetite.

Ned and Rufe O'Conner were the school bullies, and when they got after you, you either ran or got beat up. TJ Flint was small and skinny for his age. He was near-sighted and tended to squint when he didn't have his glasses on. His ears stuck out a bit, and his hair went in all directions. He was an easy target for being picked on, and Rufe and Ned

4

never missed a chance. They called him "Flint the squint" or sometimes just "Squint."

Today was the day he had to get up in front of the class and give a talk. Lately Ned and Rufe had forgotten to torment him, but TJ knew his talk would once again make him the center of their attention. It seemed cruel that this should happen on the last day of school. It spoiled the fun of getting out for summer vacation.

When he got downstairs, his mom was just taking the bacon off the stove.

"What's the matter, son?" his mother said, looking at him sharply as he pushed his bacon and eggs around on his plate. TJ had, in fact, been thinking of escape routes he could use after school.

"Not hungry, Mom. Gotta go!"

TJ's dad was just coming in from the barn to get breakfast. He was a short, dark-com-plected man who, except for startling blue eyes, might have looked like an Indian.

"What's the rush, son?" he called.

"Late, Dad, gotta run! See you after school!"

5

"Did you bring some wood in for Mom?"

"Oh yeah, Dad, I'll get it," said TJ, running for the wood box. "When can I start helping you with the trees, Dad?"

"I can sure use the help, Teej. Christmas trees are a lot of work, but I want you to take a week or two to run around and enjoy your freedom before you start working with me."

"A week will be plenty, Dad," said TJ, dumping an armload of wood in the wood box. "See you later!"

"See you, pal!"

He was off, running down through the pasture to the lane that led to the one-room country school.

TJ's talk had to be about someone he loved and admired, and TJ had chosen to talk about his granddad, Joe Tanner, who had been the chief engineer for the Green Mountain Railroad. Joe and his little steam engine had

6

both been retired when the Green Mountain had been bought out by the much larger Rutland Railroad.

TJ's granddad had a cabin up near the railroad barn. TJ had spent many a snowy Vermont evening there, stretched out on the braided rug by the old wood stove, listening to his granddad tell railroad stories. It was easy for TJ to tell the class why he loved and admired his granddad.

On the last day of school, he finished his talk by telling about the time his granddad had been peering through falling wet snow in the evening gloom and had seen a massive fir tree brought down across the tracks by the weight of the snow. He had pulled the brake lever full on, and the train had slid on the snowy tracks to within ten feet of the huge tree. It had taken him, the fireman and the brakeman three hours to clear the tracks with the saw they always carried in the engine cab.

"So that is why I admire my granddad," TJ finished up. "He saved his train lots of times. He is a brave man. I love him because he's so much fun to be with and because he's my granddad."

"A very good talk, TJ," said Miss Ridley. "I hope I get to meet your grandfather some day. He sounds like a wonderful man."

After she had dismissed the children, TJ was starting home. He still felt the warm glow of his success and had forgotten Rufe and Ned. Alas, Rufe and Ned had not forgotten *him*. Rufe was leaning up against the old pine tree in the schoolyard, his lower lip stuck out, and his long blond hair hanging across a face gone red with bad temper.

"Your granddad ain't worth nothin'!" he said. "He's just a broken-down old has-been!"

TJ had been running from the O'Conner twins since the first grade, but when he heard Rufe talking about his granddad, something happened in his head. A tingling red mist came before his eyes and, suddenly he was running right at Rufe, fists flying. He felt his fist hit Rufe's nose, then suddenly felt his arms pinned from behind as Ned pulled him off and threw him to the ground. After that, all he could see was blond lanky hair, fists and stars as the twins both punched him, but he

8

heard a shrill angry scream.

"Stop that, Ned! Stop it, Rufe! Stop it, I said!"

There was a swish, whack and a swish, whack and both twins let out a yelp, jumped off TJ and backed away holding their backsides. As TJ's head cleared, he looked up to see Sally Fisk like a small avenging angel holding a pine branch like a buggy whip.

"Get on!" she said, "or you'll get it over your heads!"

"We ain't afraid of you, Freckles," said Rufe, but he continued to back off.

"Get your books, TJ, and let's go home," Sally told him, and they started out together. Sally still had her stick.

"Next time we'll get you when you ain't got your girlfriend to protect you, Squint! We'll take you to pieces!"

"Ignore 'em, TJ," said Sally. "They're just stupid woodchucks!"

TJ had managed to hold back the tears, but just barely. He didn't feel too good. His lip was swelling, and his eye was puffed up, but as they reached his yard, Sally, who was a pretty girl in spite of her freckles, took hold of his arm and said:

"TJ, I think you were very brave to fight those boys like that," and she leaned over and gave TJ the lightest kiss on the cheek, almost like a breath.

TJ put his hand to his cheek and called:

"See you tomorrow, Sally!" but she was gone, running across the meadow toward her home, pigtails flying.

All of a sudden, TJ felt *good*. In fact, for the second time that day, he felt invulnerable. His dad rode up on the old tractor and stopped.

"You don't look so good, son, what happened?"

"Nothing much, Dad, I got in a fight."

"Looks like you lost."

"I did, Dad, but it was the O'Conner twins. Both of 'em are bigger'n me. I gave one of 'em a bloody nose."

His dad grinned as TJ ran for the kitchen.

"Wonder what his Mom'll say," he mused.

Then he heard her:

"Oh my heavens! TJ!"

2

*T*J WOKE THE NEXT MORNING AT SUNRISE. The gold morning light, turned green by the young leaves of the maple tree, outside his window, was pouring into his room. He looked at himself in the small mirror over his bureau and giggled. With two black eyes, his hair sticking out and the green light hitting him, he looked something like a crazed, green raccoon!

He pulled on his jeans, a sweatshirt and his sneakers, and easing himself carefully down the steep, narrow stairs, he let himself out the back door without waking his folks. He ran down the meadow to the woods and found the path that led to Sally's house. He knew if he got to the Fisk cabin before seven, Sally's mom would give him breakfast, and was *that* a treat! As he came out of the woods, he could see the smoke coming out of the chimney of the log cabin. When he got a little closer, the dogs set up an awful racket. They were huskies, sled dogs which Sally's dad bred and trained. There were a couple dozen of 'em, all barking at once. It made an ungodly row!

Amos Fisk, a blond, bearded giant of a man, came to the door and bellowed:

"Shut up, you dogs!" Dead silence.

"Sorry about the welcome, TJ. Twenty-two dogs are just too much. Good thing eight of 'em are sold. Come on in and get some grub. My gosh, boy, you look bunged up!"

"The O'Conner twins jumped me," said TJ, "but I gave one of 'em a bloody nose, and Sally got after 'em with a stick."

"Yeah, she told us about it. Those boys are a lot bigger than you, TJ. I think you two did real well. One of these days I just might have to teach those boys a lesson. Throw 'em up in the top of a pine tree."

As they went in the kitchen, Jane Fisk, Sally's mom, who was small, dark and energetic like Sally, said:

"Amos, I feel sorry for those boys. They

wouldn't be so tough if their father wasn't so hard on them. Tim O'Conner's been drinking too much since Martha died. It makes him mean. He treats those boys hard. Goodness, TJ, you sure look a mess! Sit down and have some pancakes and sausage." (Sally's mom made thin crispy pancakes and her homemade sausage had won prizes, so TJ didn't argue but swallowed three times as he cut into the buttered, crispy pile.)

"Mrs. Fisk, can Sally come up on Bear Mountain with me today? I know a place where you can sneak up to the bog and watch the beavers. I've got some sandwiches that Mom made last night."

"Yeah, can I Mom?" Sally chimed in. "We'll be home way before dark."

"Make sure you are, Sal. It's deep woods up there. You kids are good in the woods, but after dark, anyone could get lost up there."

"OK, Mom," Sally called, as they both ran for the door.

"I'm gonna get Pip, TJ, come on around back."

There was a box nailed up near Sally's

bedroom window with a hole in the side near the log wall. Sally made a clucking sound with her tongue, and a comical little squirrel face appeared in the hole. Quick as a flash, Pip scampered down the side of the cabin and jumped to Sally's shoulder. He flicked his long bushy tail around her neck for stability and started grooming his face. Pip had not been awake too long but was always ready for an adventure.

They started across the fields. Twenty minutes later they were at the base of Bear Mountain. TJ got the tin cup out of his pack

15

and they had a satisfying drink from Cooper's Stream. It was cold and clear; melted snow that found its way down from Bear Mountain.

After hiking up the old logging trail for almost an hour, they came to the old cemetery and decided to stop there for a rest. There were twenty or so graves covered with grass and moss, and it was restful to stretch out there with the sun dappling down through the tender June leaves.

Pip found an acorn and ran up to the first limb of a maple tree to eat it.

"Elias Crick," TJ read, "a good man and beloved father and husband, 1789-1850."

"Gosh, Sal, this man was born in the seventeen hundreds. I bet he had a farm up here."

"Up here in the woods?"

"Yeah, Dad told me all this on the lower part of the mountain used to be farmland. Look way down there in the woods, Sal, see that stone wall?" Sally could just see it.

"Yeah, I see it."

"That used to border a field. These trees are about a foot thick. Dad said they're less than a hundred years old. Back in the eighteen hundreds, all this was pastures."

"Gosh, TJ, just think of those people living way up here. It must have been hard to get to town in the wintertime."

"I don't think they went to town in the winter. If they needed something, they probably just went without it. Dad said they were a rugged bunch of folks. It's colder up here in the winter, too."

"Why do you suppose people are afraid of graveyards, TJ? I just love it here. I almost feel some kind of connection with the people who used to live up here."

"I know what you mean, Sally. It feels like a happy place to me."

After hiking for another hour, they were pretty well puffed. Finally the trail began to level off. Soon TJ saw the game trail that led to Cranberry Bog. It was almost like a tunnel

17

through the dense, young evergreens. It was hard to see the opening to it. Sally had turned away for a second and when she looked back, TJ was gone.

"TJ!" she called.

"Right down here."

Sally dropped to her knees and crawled up the trail. Limbs brushed her back, and Pip held onto her braids and chittered with concern. After they crawled about fifty yards, TJ held a finger to his lips for quiet. Carefully, they eased into a little clearing that was bedded deep with pine needles. They could see that some of the small pine trees had been gnawed by the beavers. Like Indians, they eased their heads through a fringe of underbrush to look over Cranberry Pond, which was on the lower end of the bog. As they had hoped, there was a beaver swimming toward the dam with a branch in his mouth. Sally spotted another one on the shore working away on the base of a young birch tree. While they watched the beaver work, Pip scooted to the top of the tallest pine on the edge of the clearing. They were quiet as pos-

sible for about ten minutes when suddenly TJ let out a yelp.

"Ouch! That hurt!"

A small, dense, green pine cone that had little spikes on it had bounced off TJ's head. Pip chittered with delight.

"Dang you, Pip, you did that on purpose!"

Sally collapsed in laughter.

Kersplosh! It sounded like someone had thrown a great rock into the pond. They both jumped, and Pip ran to the back side of the tree.

"Beaver smacked the water with his tail," said TJ rubbing the top of his head. "That's their warning signal. We won't see any more of them."

"Let's eat our sandwiches," said Sally. "I'm about to starve!"

They stretched out in the soft pine needles and munched their ham sandwiches. Pip insisted on a share of the oatmeal cookies and apples that TJ's mom had put in the pack. He ran up TJ's leg, sat on his knee and scolded until TJ broke off some tidbits to keep him quiet.

"You don't know how to be a proper squirrel," TJ said. "Squirrels are supposed to be shy with people, but you're a bossy little stinker."

Sally giggled.

"Isn't he, though! I guess I must have spoiled him."

On the way home, they had just reached the edge of the woods near TJ's house when they heard a dog barking.

"That sounds like Babe," TJ said. "What in the world is she after?"

The barking was continuous and it caused TJ and Sally to run down the wood line to see what was going on. Sure enough, there was Babe, the Flint's old golden retriever, sitting on her haunches barking her head off.

"Babe, what's going on, girl?"

TJ ran up, and, as he approached, Babe got up and went into the woods. TJ followed her to what looked like a large dead animal.

"Look at this, Sal. I think it's a dead wolf! It's huge! It must be over a hundred pounds. There's blood, Sal."

"Yeah, TJ, looks like somebody shot him."

As they knelt beside the dead animal to get a better look, they found themselves looking into a bright, amber eye.

It blinked!

3

*"H*E'S ALIVE, TJ!"

"Yeah, he is! Can you see him breathing?"

"I think so, just barely."

"Listen, Sal, I'm gonna run get my dad."

"I'll get my dad too, TJ, he's really good at doctoring dogs. I'll meet you back here as soon as I can. You better bring the garden cart. Put some straw in it."

"I will, Sal. See you in a little while!"

Amos Fisk and Sally got back first, and Amos was pulling on heavy leather training gloves and kneeling down, when John Flint and TJ arrived, out of breath, with the garden cart.

"He's not a wolf, kids," said Amos, "he's a dog, an Alaskan malamute, but I bet you he's got some wolf in him. Man, he's big! If this dog was in shape, he'd weigh a hundred and twenty pounds. Most malamutes only go around eighty or eighty-five pounds. This guy is the biggest malamute I've ever seen. He's a young dog, too. Maybe two or three years old."

"Is he gonna die, Dad?"

"Don't know yet, Sal. Let me see if I can touch him."

"All right, big fellow. Easy...I'm not gonna hurt you..."

Very slowly he reached out his gloved hand to the big dog's muzzle. The dog gave a little whining sigh and licked the glove.

"He's tame, kids. This big, mean-looking guy is tame as a pussycat!" He pulled off his gloves and gently began to stroke the dog's ear, talking softly all the time.

"It's OK, boy. Not gonna hurt you. OK, now..."

"He's been shot, alright. Belly wound. Can't tell for sure in this light, but it doesn't look too deep. He's lost blood. Looks like he might have been pretty worn out before he ever got shot. His pads are all knicked up. He's come a long way on rough ground. Hasn't had much to eat. I'm not sure, but if we can get him someplace warm and get this wound cleaned up and get some broth down him, he might come around."

John Flint moved the garden cart into position, and they unfolded an old blanket he had brought.

"Let's see if we can get him in the cart," he said.

"I'll take his head with my gloves on," said Amos. "He might try to bite if we hurt him."

Carefully, they eased the big dog onto the blanket, and by lifting the blanket, they got him into the bed of straw in the garden cart. Once again he tried to lick Amos' gloved hand.

"This is a good dog," said Amos. "He knows we're trying to help him."

When they got back to the Flint house, Betsy brought some hot water and clean rags outside so that Amos could work on the dog in the daylight. Again, he showed no sign of trying to bite. As he cleaned the wound, Amos said:

"Just what I thought. It's not bad, only a graze. I think he's mostly just starved and exhausted. Let's get him inside."

They carried him to the stove where Betsy had folded up an old quilt. Sally and TJ supported the dog's head, and he was able to lap some warm broth.

"This old boy needs to have a small amount of broth every half hour," Amos said. "Somebody needs to stay with him all night." TJ and Sally started to talk at once:

"Can I stay up with him Mom, can I?"

"Can I stay and help TJ, Dad?"

Betsy Flint looked at Amos.

"You kids think you could stay awake?" Amos said.

"Sure Dad. We can take turns sleeping. We'll do a good job."

"We sure will!" said TJ.

"Well, I don't see why not," said Betsy. "What do you think, John?"

"OK, kids," John said. "You've got nurse

25

duty. Someone has got to take care of this guy."

That night after dinner, TJ could barely take his eyes off the big dog.

"Can we keep him, Dad? I think he's gonna be a really good dog."

"Well, TJ, maybe so. Babe is getting pretty old, and when I'm out in the fields working, I like to know there's a big dog at home that could be some protection. If he likes us when he gets better, and if nobody shows up to claim him, we'll keep him."

"Wow!" said TJ, "Now we've gotta get a name. I've been thinking, his coat is kind of silver grey. What about 'Silver'?"

"That's good," said Sally through a mouthful of roast chicken. She swallowed and turned toward the stove.

"Silver," she called softly. The dog's ears came up.

C H A P T E R   3

"Welcome to the family, Silver" ! said Betsy.

But it wasn't that easy to stay up. They had been up Bear Mountain and back, and now they'd had a big chicken dinner. The idea of staying up had seemed exciting, but, by nine o'clock, they were both ready for some sleep. Sally said she thought she could make it 'til midnight so TJ got on the sofa under a blanket and was quickly asleep. Sally sat under the light at the kitchen table and tried to read. She rested her chin on her left hand, but from time to time she would doze off, only to be woken with a jerk as her head began to fall. It took forever for midnight to come, but finally she was able to wake TJ and crawl under the blanket for some sleep.

By three a.m., when it was time to wake Sally, the broth was gone. The dog was breathing deeply and sleeping well, so TJ

27

stretched out on part of the folded quilt and went to sleep.

He woke at first light to feel a warm tongue on the back of his neck. He rolled over to stare into two amber eyes, then he got the tongue on his nose which made him giggle.

"Morning, Silver," he said.

C H A P T E R   3

4

*T*HE NEXT DAY THE BIG DOG WAS ABLE TO GET on his feet and go out and make use of a tree. After three days of good food and rest, he was able to follow his new friend Babe around the yard and check out all the interesting smells. Soon, he was putting on weight. He kept pretty close to TJ but wouldn't follow if told to stay put.

The night before TJ was going to start working with his dad, TJ's folks were sitting together after dinner on the old blue kitchen sofa. His dad was worrying about the tree farm.

"Betsy, I sure hope I did the right thing raising Christmas trees on this farm. It's a good thing we have a crop ready for this year, because the money is just about gone."

"You did right, John. It's just hard waiting for that first crop. Once we get some money in this Christmas, we ought to be OK. As long as you replant, you'll get a crop every year. We'll never get rich, but just think of the happiness we'll be bringing to people at Christmas time."

"I know, Betsy, I just worry sometimes. Something could happen to the trees. A disease, or something. I don't think it will, though, the trees look beautiful. I just love this farm so much that I worry about the possibility of losing it. Any kind of farming is risky, though. I guess it's worth some risk to be able to do what you want to do. I got an idea this morning, Bets. You know, the churches in Twin Forks all sell Christmas trees to make money. If I could sign them up, they could take our whole crop. Father Denis is calling the other ministers, and I'm gonna throw a couple of trees in the truck and drive down and meet with 'em on Saturday. Why don't you and TJ come along for the ride?"

"That's a wonderful idea, John. I guess we'd use the railroad to haul the trees into Twin Forks."

"Right, Bets. All we'd have to do would

31

be get the trees to the Masonville station, get 'em loaded on flatcars and the railroad would do the rest."

"Do you want to come, TJ?" Betsy asked.

"What, Mom?" said TJ, who had been listening to Jack Benny on the radio.

"Do you want to ride into Twin Forks with me and Dad on Saturday?"

"I was gonna ask if Sally and I could go over to Granddad's on Saturday, Mom. We want to show him Silver, and he said if we brought our sleeping bags, we could spend the night in the old caboose."

"That sounds like fun, TJ. You better telephone him. If he knows for sure you're coming, he'll cook enough dinner to feed you two."

"Great Mom! I'll call him right now."

On Thursday, TJ stopped work early so he could go into Masonville to the general store and get some dog food and some groceries his mom needed. He went home first to pick up Silver. After he got some milk and cookies and a shopping list from his mom, he shrugged into his backpack, jumped the back steps and ran across the yard with Silver bounding alongside. It was about a mile to the village, so TJ slowed down and took his time on the walk. It was a beautiful day, and he was enjoying watching Silver trying to catch field mice. Silver would snurf around in the tall meadow grass in the fields along the road and then pounce with his front legs stiff and both paws coming down on a likely look-ing spot. So far, he had caught nothing. TJ was grinning at the performance.

"Silver, the mighty hunter!" he said.

Hearing his name, Silver's ears came to a point, and he tilted his head trying to under-stand.

"You'd need about twenty mice for a meal, boy, and you haven't caught even one. Good thing I'm going to buy some dog food."

Silver, pleased to be spoken to, trotted over and gave TJ's hand a lick. As they rounded

33

the bend in the dirt road and came to the plank bridge over Cooper's Stream, TJ saw that Rufe and Ned were leaning against the railing of the bridge. As usual, they looked belligerent.

"Look who's here," said Ned. "Flint the Squint! Is that mangy dog yours, Squint? Looks like the kind of miserable dog you'd have." TJ kept walking.

"You ain't got your girlfriend with her stick to protect you now, have you, Squint?" said Rufe. "I'm gonna see if I can knock some of that squint off that stupid face of yours. Grab him by the ears, Ned, and hold his head still."

TJ was feeling very hollow just under his ribs and having trouble getting his breath. Silver lay down in the road with his head between his paws.

"You guys leave me alone. I'm not bothering you."

"We'll leave you alone when we finish with you, Squint," said Rufe. "I'm gonna fix you for hittin' me in the nose. I'm gonna fix you so you won't never dare *hit* me again."

34   He reached out for TJ and grabbed his

shirt. There was a low rumbling growl. Silver's back end was off the ground, but his head was still low. His upper lip was curled showing about an inch and a half of gleaming white fang. His ears were laid flat, and the hair on the back of his neck was standing up about four inches. Rufe quickly drew back his hand.

"Look at that dog, Ned! He's *mean* looking! Does he bite?" he asked TJ.

"Not me, he doesn't," said TJ truthfully. "I don't think he likes you, though, Rufe."

"Go on, Rufe, hit him!" said Ned.

Rufe reached for TJ again, but the growl turned to a snarl and Silver crept forward. Rufe drew back.

"Not *me*! You hit him, Ned!"

The twins now seemed mad at each other. Both had forgotten TJ and were warily watching the big dog.

"Well, while you two guys argue about it, I guess we'll go on," said TJ, trying to keep from smiling. "Silver's really a nice dog. Wouldn't hurt a flea."

He bent down and gave Silver a hug and

got his face licked.

"See."

As they moved on down the road, TJ could still hear them arguing.

"Why didn't you hit him? You scared of a dog?"

"Did you see the size of that dog? Why didn't *you* hit him if you're so brave..."

"*Thanks*, Silver," said TJ.

Silver smiled at him.

C H A P T E R   4

5

---

*S*ATURDAY MORNING A PECULIAR SOUND woke Sally with a start. It sounded like dry twigs rattling on the windowpane. In the early morning light Sally could just make out Pip, front paws scrabbling on the glass, trying to dig his way through the windowpane.

"You little devil," Sally said, laughing at how hard he was working. "You scared me."

Sally raised the window a few inches, and Pip scrambled in, ran straight to the foot of the bed and took a flying leap to the desk where Sally kept the big jar of sunflower seeds. There was no lid, and Pip jumped to the mouth of the jar and tried to hold on to the edge of the opening while his back feet tried in vain to climb the slippery glass. He fell with a thump to the top of the desk, shook himself and jumped again. This time he jumped too far and fell headfirst into the jar.

When he sat up, there were sunflower shells stuck to his nose. The whole performance was so comical that Sally got a serious case of the giggles.

"Serves you right, Pip! Anybody that greedy deserves to fall on their head!"

After he loaded up his cheek pouches with seeds, Sally tipped the jar and Pip hopped out on the desk. She picked him up and put him back out the window.

"Out you go, Pip. You have to eat those seeds in *your* house. If you ate in here, you'd have shells all over the place."

40

C H A P T E R   5

With his usual good timing, TJ got to Sally's house just in time for breakfast. After they all ate, Amos went out to look at Silver.

"You did a good job on this guy, TJ. He's put on weight, and his coat is starting to shine. He looks good. Nice goin'. Jane! Come see Silver."

Jane came with a scrap of bacon which Silver accepted politely. She bent down and stroked both ears and promptly got kissed.

"This dog's a real sweetie," she said.

"He*s*, Mrs. Fisk," said TJ, "but he can be tough too."

"I bumped into Rufe and Ned on Thursday, and they still wanted to beat me up. Silver didn't like that idea too much, though, and he sure told 'em how he felt. They kind of had a change of heart about the whole business." He told them everything that happened.

"...so seeing that I'm small and Ned and

Rufe are big, I guess it's a good thing that I have friends like Sally and Silver."

"Yeah, TJ," Amos said. "A man needs good friends. Look at that!"

While they were talking, Silver had picked up an old dog harness that was lying near the barn, brought it to TJ and dropped it at his feet.

"This dog's been a sled dog! He wants to get in harness! Let's try him out on the small training sled."

Amos slipped the harness on Silver, who was wagging all over with excitement. Sally brought the training sled from the barn, and Amos showed TJ how it worked.

"See, I have this sled on wheels so you can train without snow. This brake lever is spring-loaded. It keeps friction on the back wheels to stop the sled from running too fast and hitting the dog on his back legs. Hold up on this lever and the brake starts to come off. You can control just how hard the dog has to pull by how much brake you leave on. This would be great for building Silver's strength. You can give a dog a real workout on flat

42

ground by making him work against the brake. Let's try him out."

Silver, ears forward, was quivering with excitement.

Amos showed TJ how to stand on the sled and how much pressure to keep on the brake lever.

"Try the commands 'mush on' for 'go' and 'ho' for 'stop.' We don't know what he was trained on so we'll have to see what works. Hang on when you say 'mush', 'cause an excited dog will really jump out. Go ahead. Give him a try."

"Mush on!" said TJ and his head snapped back as the sled almost flew from under his feet. The sled was across the yard and a hundred feet down the dirt road before TJ thought to add more brake and shout "ho!". The big dog stopped at once and stood looking back at TJ, tail wagging, looked pleased with himself.

"Wow!" said TJ. "That was fun!"

"He was looking back at you," Amos said. "I believe he was checking for hand signals. Some folks use 'gee' and 'haw' for 'right' and 'left', but I prefer hand signals. Take him up

43

the road to the fork and when he looks at you, point the way you want him to go. Point with your whole arm. When you want to come back, stop him then take him by the collar and face him in the other direction."

This time TJ was prepared for the quick start. They saw him disappear around the bend in a small cloud of dust. In a minute, they were back. As they approached the drive, TJ pointed left and Silver obeyed, pulling the sled up to the Fisk log cabin.

"That's a smart dog," said Amos. "Somebody did a good job training him. There's not much I can teach him about pulling a sled. He loves to do it, too. That's the sign of a good sled dog."

"Can we take the sled over to Mr. Tanner's, Dad?" Sally asked. "It's about two miles. Is that too far for him to pull us?"

"I don't think so, Sal. That dog's looking pretty strong, and the road's flat over that way. Just go light on the brake. If he starts to look tired, give him a rest."

"Is it safe, Amos?" said Sally's mom. "Could he run off with 'em or something?"

"He could, Janie, but he won't. That's a good dog. He's calm and steady. You don't have to worry about *him*.

"You kids can put the sleeping bags in the sled. Sally can sit on 'em and TJ can stand on the back and drive."

They loaded up the sled, and both kids climbed aboard.

"This," said TJ, "is the way to travel."

"Mush on, Silver!"

Out the drive they flew!

C H A P T E R   5

6

*T*J'S GRANDDAD WAS JUST GOING INTO THE cabin with an armload of stove wood when he saw the dogsled coming up the road.

"Whooee, Rocky!" he called into the cabin. "Come look at this!" A short, powerful looking black man came out on the porch.

"What's up, Joe? Oh my. Looks like we done had some invisible snow! Those your grandchildren?"

"One of 'em is. The boy. Little girl's his friend."

"Ho, Silver!" TJ yelled as the sled pulled up to the cabin porch.

"Hey, Granddad! What do you think of this?"

"I wish I'd had such a thing when I was your age. Looks like fun."

"It is, Mr. Tanner," said Sally. "It's more fun than anything!"

47

"That is one pretty dog, TJ. You said you call him 'Silver' ?"

"Yes sir. On account of his coat."

"Kids, I want you to meet Mr. Rockland. He and I worked together on the Santa Fe Railroad years ago. He was the best fireman I ever worked with. Rocky, this is my grandson, TJ, and his friend Sally."

"Hi, kids. You can call me Rocky. Any friend of Joe's is a friend of mine." He stuck out a huge, work-hardened hand and kneeled down in front of Silver.

"Hey, boy. Ain't you pretty."

Silver held out a paw in greeting.

"I like this guy."

"He likes you, Mr... Rocky."

"Kids, years ago, your granddad and I used to be quite a team. We were best friends, but I got transferred to another run, and we lost touch with each other. When I retired, I found out your granddad had moved up here, so I decided to come pay him a visit. That was a couple weeks ago, and here I still am. We're having so much fun, I just may never leave!"

48

"Hope you don't, Rocky. I sure do enjoy

having some company. Anyway, you said you wouldn't leave until you beat me in checkers. That means you'll be here permanently."

"Ha! We'll see about that! Tonight's the night, Joe. Tonight's the night."

"I can beat Granddad, Rocky," said TJ. "Let's play him together."

"No fair gangin' up, you two," said Joe. "If that's gonna be the deal, I want Sally on my side."

Sally had unharnessed Silver and was starting up a game of tag with him, running away as fast as she could.

"Don't, Sal!" yelled TJ. "He'll knock you... oops!"

"Uff!" said Sally as her breath went out. Silver had launched his body at the back of Sally's legs, knocking her flat on the grass.

"See that, Joe? He *clipped* her!" said Rocky. "That's a foul in football."

"Silver doesn't know about football," said TJ. "That's the way he thinks you play tag. You all right, Sal?"

Silver stood over Sally, trying to get her

breath. "He sure did tag me!"

"He loves tag," said TJ, "but nobody wants to play with him more than once. Sorry, Sal. I tried to warn you, but I wasn't quick enough."

"I'm too old for tag," said Rocky.

"Me too!" said Sally.

That night, after finishing one of Joe's savory stews, they all sat on the cabin porch. Rocky got his guitar and sang a couple of railroad songs. He was good, and TJ and Sally wanted more, but Rocky put the guitar aside.

"You kids know me and Joe here worked together on the Santa Fe Railroad out west years ago. Well, did you ever hear about the time we stopped a train robbery?" Both kids clamored for the story, while Rocky leaned back in the porch swing and lit his pipe.

"Well, see, this was way back in the winter of nineteen hundred. We were on a westward run out of Santa Fe. We were pulling some

51

cattle and some freight cars, but we also had a mail car with a Wells Fargo cash shipment. That must have been what them robbers were after. Whatever they wanted they didn't get it.

"See, there was a curved stretch of track leading to a trestle that went over a gorge. We always slowed there. We never liked to take that curve more'n ten miles an hour 'cause the road bed was rough there, and we sure didn't want to derail and end up down in that gorge. The robbers must have known we slowed there 'cause that's where they were layin' for us. Joe always had his eyes peeled, and he saw the sun strike a rifle barrel up ahead. He *hollered* at me:

'Trouble Rocky! Keep your head down and put the coal to her!' Then he hit the throttle."

Joe interrupted:

"Rocky, you were shoveling so fast your arms were a blur!"

"*Yeah* I was!"

Rocky went on.

"They musta had their horses hid up in a draw, 'cause when they saw us speedin' up, they came out full tilt ridin' alongside the train, tryin' to swing aboard. I guess there were five or six of 'em. By that time we were doin' thirty miles an hour, and they couldn't make it. They must a been kind a angry 'cause they pulled up and started shootin'. Bullets were whangin' off the cab, and me and Joe was all scrunched down out of sight."

Joe said:

"Rocky, I always figured we hit that trestle doing forty. I still don't know why we didn't go down in the gorge. At that speed, we should have jumped the tracks."

"Yeah, Joe, we were lucky. I never thought we'd make it."

TJ and Sally were excited.

"Gosh, Granddad," TJ said, "I wish I'd known that story when I told the class about you. You really *were* a hero!"

"You sure were, Mr. Tanner!" said Sally.

"Well, kids, for a hero, I sure did a whole lot of duckin' and runnin' away."

"That ain't all you did, Joe," said Rocky. "You did something a whole lot better than that. *You seen the rifle barrel.*"

53

Soon they were all trying not to yawn. TJ's granddad lit a kerosene lantern and they all walked down the dirt road to the tracks. Further on, the tracks of the siding ran into a barn which sheltered the old steam engine. Joe kept the caboose and the engine shined up and in working order even though they were no longer being used by the railroad. Joe said he's been around engines so long that it wouldn't feel right not to be working on one.

They climbed into the little red caboose and lit the shiny brass oil lamp that hung from the ceiling. There were three bunks. TJ and Sally each selected one and rolled out their sleeping bags. There was a neat little stove and a booth with seats on either side of a table. Joe had put up little red curtains to make it more homelike. All in all, it was very cozy.

"Makes you feel right at home, don't it,

54

Rocky?"

"Sure does, Joe. Listen, you kids be sure to lock up good. Sometimes hobos show up around here. Most of 'em are harmless, but some ain't too nice. Reckon they're safe sleepin' out here, Joe?"

"You forget who's with 'em, Rocky? There's not many hobos would like to tangle with Silver."

"You're right Joe. The fort's secure. Get up here, boy." Rocky patted the third bunk, and Silver jumped up and settled down looking pleased.

After Joe and Rocky went back to the cabin, Sally blew out the oil lamp, and snuggled down in her sleeping bag.

"I sure do like Rocky, TJ. He's an awful lot of fun."

"Me too, Sal. I hope he stays. I think Granddad's been kind of lonely living alone. Now he's got his best friend with him."

"Hasn't this been a wonderful summer, TJ?"

"It sure has, Sal," came the sleepy reply. "It sure *has*!"

55

7

*A*S THE SUMMER HURRIED ON TO FALL, TJ and Sally had lots of adventures with Silver. During the week TJ worked with his dad pruning the Christmas trees that were ready for harvest and planting more young trees. While they were working, Silver stayed home and kept an eye on the farm. Babe, the old golden retriever, who was too old and lazy for adventures, seemed to enjoy the company. On weekends, Sally would usually come over and they would harness up Silver, take some sandwiches and head out looking for adventure.

One Saturday, Sally came over with Pip. She was worried that Silver's hunting instincts would come out when he saw the squirrel, but, though Pip scolded loudly from Sally's shoulder, the big dog ignored him with lordly disdain. He seemed to think it would be beneath him to recognize a squirrel.

Silver loved to pull the sled. The people

around Masonville got used to seeing TJ, Sally and Pip being pulled by the malamute and would grin and wave with pleasure. Everyone but the O'Conner twins, that is. Ned and Rufe were afraid to get too close but never missed a chance to yell insults at TJ, calling him "Squint" and jeering about his "freckled girlfriend" and his "mangy dog." It was on a Saturday, late in August, when TJ and Sally had their biggest adventure.

They were in the sled coming back from TJ's granddad's cabin. When they passed some woods near Bear Mountain, TJ thought he heard something.

"Ho, Silver!" he said. "Did you hear something, Sal? Wait a minute, there it is again!" It was very faint, but it sounded like "help".

"Is someone yelling 'help'?" said TJ.

"Yeah. Sounds like that to me. Aren't there some cliffs back there behind those trees?"

"Yeah. Me and Dad used to climb 'em. Come on Sal, we better see if someone's in trouble. *Stay*, Silver!"

They ran through the woods, jumped a little creek and came out at the base of the cliff. On the face of the cliff, about twenty feet off the ground, on a six-inch ledge, hanging on with his fingertips and whimpering with fear was one of the O'Conner twins. Almost below him, curled up holding his ankle and groaning was the other twin.

"My gosh, did you guys try to climb that cliff without ropes?" said TJ.

"Ned's broke his leg, and I can't get down," moaned Rufe from the cliff. "If I move, I'll fall like Ned did. You gotta get help, Squint."

"OK, OK, let me think," said TJ. "Just relax, Rufe, and hang on. If you don't move, you won't fall."

"Your granddad's place is the only place near here," said Sally, "but him and Rocky aren't there."

"Yeah, I know. Listen, Sal, you stay here with Ned. I'm gonna take Silver back to Granddad's and get a coil of rope. If we have rope, I think we can get Rufe off the cliff. I can telephone from Granddad's. Mom and Dad will help us. Maybe they can get Dr.

James. I'll be back as soon as I can." He was off, sprinting through the woods.

Sally went over to Ned, whose eyes were glazed with shock. He had a big bump on his head and some scrapes, but his ankle seemed to be the worst. She eased his pants leg up to look. It looked bad. Blue and badly swollen. His foot was at a funny angle. Sally, who had never seen a broken leg before, was sure she was looking at one. There wasn't much she could do. She had a sweatshirt tied around her waist. She took it off and folded it to make a little pillow and slipped it under Ned's head. He looked up at Sally, brown eyes dark and scared in his pale, bruised face, teeth clenched against the pain.

"Thanks," he gasped.

Sally heard TJ coming back through the woods. As he approached the cliff, she could see that he had a coil of rope.

"That was quick," said Sally.

"Yeah, I let Silver run flat out. Almost flipped the sled a couple of times. We really flew.

"Listen Sal, we gotta gct to the top of the cliff. Rufe, can you hold on a little longer?"

"Yeah," said Rufe, "but hurry. My leg is startin' to cramp."

Sally and TJ ran through the woods to where the ridge tapered off. Soon they had worked their way up the ridge to the top of the cliff. TJ walked carefully to the edge and soon found a place where he could look down on Rufe. He uncoiled the rope and tied a loop in it leaving about ten feet of rope below the loop. Then he walked back and took two turns around a pine tree.

"Sal, you gotta let me down to Rufe. The friction of the rope around the tree will take most of the strain. Let me down slow 'til I

yell 'stop,' and I'll get the end tied around
Rufe. When I'm ready, I'll yell 'down!' and
you can let us down the rest of the way. Just
don't let the rope out too fast, OK?"

"OK, TJ. Let's go."

TJ went to the edge of the cliff, slipped the
loop over his body and began to climb down.
Sally let the rope out as he went, ready to take
the strain if he fell. A rock slid under TJ's
foot and suddenly the rope went tight. Sally
held it easily as the two coils bit into the pine
tree.

"OK, TJ?" she yelled.

"OK, now, give me some more!" Again,
she began to let the rope slide around the tree.

"Stop!" TJ was on the ledge with Rufe.

He worked his way over to Rufe, reached
around him with the line and tied a knot leaving a loop around Rufe's body.

"OK now, Rufe, hold on to me and start to
climb down. If you slip, the rope'll catch
you."

"You sure?" said Rufe. "That little girl's
holdin' the rope? She ain't too strong."

"She was strong enough to run you off

63

with a pine branch! Just do what I said. The rope is wrapped around a tree. She's gonna let us down real slow."

Very slowly, Rufe transferred his grip to TJ and, holding him tightly began to climb off the ledge. As the rope took the strain, TJ heard his dad calling:

"TJ! Where are you?"

"Over here, Dad! On the cliff! Let us down, Sal! Slow!"

John Flint and Dr. James came out of the woods in time to see Rufe and TJ half dangling, half climbing down the face of the cliff. Dr. James ran to Ned, and TJ's dad came to the bottom of the cliff and helped the boys get on solid ground.

"Good job, TJ! Is Sally up top?"

"Thanks, Dad. Yeah, she let us down. Rufe was stuck. Ned fell."

Rufe was sitting down with his head resting on his bent knees.

"You OK, Rufe?" asked John Flint.

"Yeah, but Ned's hurt."

"How's he doin', Ben?" John Flint asked

Dr. James.

"He'll be all right, John. Mild concussion. Broken ankle. We'll have to carry him out to the truck. I'll set his leg back at your house."

After Sally got down, they carried Ned to the truck and got him on an old mattress John Flint had put in the back. Dr. James and Rufe got in the back with Ned, and Dr. James gave him a shot of morphine for the pain.

Sally and TJ came over to the truck.

"Dad, me and Sally will come back with Silver and the sled."

"OK, son, we'll see you at home."

"Squint," said Rufe. "I owe you a big one. You *and* Freckles. You two saved me from a bad fall, and you got help for Ned."

"Yeah, Rufe. Well, you can pay us back by never callin' us 'Squint' and 'Freckles' again."

Rufe looked at them, his eyes filled up with tears and his mouth pulled down at the corners.

"*Thanks*, TJ," he said. "*Thanks*, Sally."

8

*T*HE REEK OF ETHER FILLED THE FLINT HOUSE,
driving out the homey odors with its sickening, sweet smell. Betsy Flint came down
from TJ's bedroom where she had held the
wire-mesh mask over Ned's mouth and nose
while Dr. James had carefully dripped ether
on the mask to put him to sleep. She went
around the house throwing open windows and
doors. It was a breezy day, and the smell
began to clear.

"Awful stuff, TJ! I thought it was going to
knock me out, leaning over the mask and
smelling those fumes. Ugh!" She looked pale
and ill.

They heard the Ford truck pull up outside
and stop. John Flint came in followed by Mr.
O'Conner. Tim O'Conner's bloodshot eyes
gave his angry, worried expression a kind of
wild look. Dr. James was coming down the
stairs wiping plaster off his hands.

"He's coming 'round. Somebody needs to be with him to make sure he doesn't thrash around while the cast sets up. He'll be confused for a while, too, and he may throw up from the ether." He spoke to Tim O'Conner:

"Hello, Tim, why don't you go on up. Your other boy's up there with him now. Ned's gonna be fine when his leg mends. He was lucky. That fall could've killed him." Tim grabbed his hand and shook it.

"Thanks, Doc. I sure do appreciate it!" He turned loose and headed for the stairs following John Flint to the bedroom.

"Can you handle the nursing, Betsy? I got some other calls to make."

"Sure, Ben. We'll take care of him. Thanks again for coming so quick."

"You did good with the ether mask. Want a job as my operating room nurse?" He fished around in his black bag and came out with a small bottle of pills.

"Ugh! No thanks! I'd never get used to the smell of that stuff." She took the pills from Doc.

"Ha!" said Doc. "You're right. You never

do get used to it. Give him one of those pills every four hours for pain."

"OK, Ben. Thanks again."

Upstairs, Tim O'Conner followed John into the bedroom. Rufe was sitting by the bed looking scared. Ned was moaning and waking up.

"Don't whip me Daddy," he begged, his eyes still closed. Tears began to run down his cheeks. "I'm sorry, Daddy. I won't climb up there no more. *Don't* whip me."

Tim O'Conner knelt by the bed and took Ned's hand. He patted it.

"It's all right son," he said. "I'm right here. It's all right. I ain't never gonna whip you again." He looked at Rufe. "I ain't *never* gonna whip *neither* of you boys again!"

C H A P T E R   8

9

*O*N SEPTEMBER 3RD, THE FIRST DAY OF school, TJ awoke, as usual, to the smell of bacon frying. There was something else in the air, too. TJ sniffed. Something tangy and crisp like the taste of cider... Fall! He sat up and looked out of his window and, sure enough, some of the maple trees had a dusting of bright yellow and crimson. There was no humidity, and the sky was a clear, deep blue.

TJ knew he was very happy about school, then he realized why. For the first time in years, he was going to be able to go to school without worrying about the O'Conner twins. Now they were his friends. He'd be in the fourth grade, but it didn't make much difference. It was a one-room school, so he'd be back in the same room with Miss Ridley. This was fine with TJ, because he liked Miss Ridley a lot. Of course, Sally would be there, along with the James kids and the Grundy kids. There was supposed to be a new boy, too. Bob Hanson, or Hampton...something like that. TJ hadn't met him.

As TJ polished off his eggs and bacon, Betsy Flint slid two more slices of hot toast on his plate.

"Nothing wrong with your appetite, TJ."

"No, Mom, I think I could've eaten a skunk this morning."

"Glad you didn't have to," she said with a grin. "Eggs are better."

"You better explain to Silver about his staying with me while you're in school." Silver, hearing his name, cocked his head.

"Silver," TJ said, "you gotta stay with Mom. I'll be back this afternoon."

Silver looked worried as TJ left for school. He stood at the screen door watching TJ run across the yard. Babe got up from her bed beside the stove and came to the door to watch.

"OK, you two," Betsy said to the dogs, breaking a piece of bacon in half. "Here's a treat."

C H A P T E R   9

The weather stayed beautiful, and the kids had had their lunch in the schoolyard. TJ and Tommy James were having a game of stretch.

TJ flipped his pocketknife into the grass, and it stuck about six inches from Tommy's foot. Tommy moved his foot over to the knife, retrieved it and, legs spread wide, trying to keep his balance, flipped it a few inches from TJ's foot. TJ tried to make the stretch but his feet were too far apart and he fell over.

"Good game, Tommy," he said as the new boy, Bob Hampton, came up. Bob was in TJ's grade, but he was big, tough-looking and not too friendly. TJ stood up and stuck out his hand to the new boy.

"Hi, I'm TJ," he said.

"You sure are a funny looking little runt," said Bob with a sneer, ignoring TJ's hand.

"Oh, boy," said TJ. "Here we go again."

"Hey you, new boy! Come over here!" It

was Rufe, over by the schoolhouse. Bob strolled over trying to look casual.

"What you want?" he said.

"What's your name?" said Rufe.

"Name's Bob."

"Listen, Bob," said Rufe. "Here's some advice. That kid you were talking to over there is a tough little guy. He gave me a bloody nose." Bob looked doubtful.

"That's true," said Ned. "I seen it. Here's something else. That kid is TJ Flint, and he has the biggest dog in Vermont. It's half wolf. If you mess with TJ, that dog will surely chew your ears off."

"That's right," said Rufe, "and if the dog don't chew 'em off, *we will*. TJ is a very special friend of ours. Is this comin' clear to you, Bob?"

(Ned had started to laugh at the thought of chewing on Bob's ears.)

"Yeah, sure. I don't want no trouble."

"That's it, Bob," said Ned, trying not to laugh. "No trouble. This is a little school. Everybody needs to get along good. We don't stand for no bullyin'."

"I get it," said Bob. "Don't worry. I'm friendly, real friendly."

Miss Ridley, standing nearby, heard this exchange and shook her head in amazement.

"Ned and Rufe won't allow bullying!" she thought. "Will wonders never cease!"

10

*I*T WAS SATURDAY, THE FIRST DAY OF OCT-
ober, and the woods were ablaze with color.
The dark green pines and cedars looked
almost black against the crimson, pinkish-
orange, yellow, gold and green of the hard-
wood trees. There had been a frost the night
before, and the crisp air foretold another on
the way.

The Flints were having a potluck supper
that night, and Betsy's wood-burning cook
stove was filling the house with the smells of
homemade bread, apples and cinnamon. Joe
and Rocky were going to bring one of Joe's
famous beef stews, and Jane Fisk, Sally's
mom, was going to bring a vegetable casse-
role. Tim O'Conner, who wasn't much of a
cook, had promised to stop by Grundy's cider
mill and pick up a couple of gallons of fresh-
squeezed cider. They were all going to talk

74

over the Christmas tree harvest.

John Flint had been in the woods most of
the day splitting firewood, and TJ had worked
with him, helping to stack the wood on the
flatbed trailer that hitched behind their old
tractor. It was almost dark by five, and Betsy
was not surprised to hear them coming into
the mud room to pull off their coats, boots and
gloves.

"*Boy,* TJ! Does that smell good!"

"Better'n that, Dad, that smells *wonderful*!"

Betsy found her stove surrounded: man,
boy and two dogs.

"What a bunch of moochers," she said, taking two loaves out of the oven. "This bread's
for supper, but I'll give you one small sample
each." She cut off the heel, gave half to each
dog and cut two pieces for man and boy, slapping soft butter on each slice.

"Thanks, Mom," said TJ, butter dripping
down his chin. "It's *good*. I'm going up and
listen to Jack Armstrong."

John Flint flopped on the blue sofa.

"Pooped!" he said. "*Man*, that bread's
worth dying for! You sure have the touch,

Honey."

Betsy's face lit with pleasure.

"I bet you say that to all the girls," she said.

"Ain't got no other girls," he said, patting the sofa. "Come sit with me a minute, and give me a kiss."

Upstairs, TJ flopped on his bed and invited Silver to join him. He snapped on his little radio and for a half hour was lost in the adventures of "Terry and The Pirates" and "Jack Armstrong." Silver dozed. Soon, he heard the Fisks arrive. He called down to Sally.

"Come on up, Sal. There's some good stuff on the radio."

Silver, whining with pleasure, ran to meet her at the top of the stairs and got a big hug.

"Silver! Hey boy! You look beautiful! Yeah, I'm glad to see you, too!" She climbed into TJ's chair.

"Wow, you got a new Walt Disney," she said. "I love comics."

"Me too, Sal, and I love books, too. You read much?"

"Yeah, TJ, but I think I like the boys books better than the girls books. More adventures in 'em. *Treasure Island's* great. You read *Penrod*?"

"Dad's been reading that to us after dinner. He reads a chapter every night. It's really funny. Last winter, when I had the mumps, Mom got me started on *The Wind in the Willows*. Boy, *that's* a wonderful book. You read it?"

"No, can I borrow it?" said Sally.

"Sure," said TJ, pulling it out of the book-shelf. "Come on, let's go down. I think I heard Granddad."

Rocky and Joe Tanner had left their coats in the mud room and were just coming into the kitchen. Joe had a big, black iron pot with a lid.

"Hey, everybody," said Rocky, "here's the world's biggest beef stew. Joe had me peeling potatoes and onions all morning. I'm just about wore out! Got a soft chair by the fire for a tired old man, John?"

"Sure do, Rocky. One for Joe, too. You gents take a load off." The O'Conners came in carrying two jugs of cider. Sally and TJ went over to say hello. The twins' new attitude had been so friendly that there was no longer any strain between the four of them. Even Silver was treating Ned and Rufe as friends.

"This old dog really is nice once you get to know him," said Rufe.

"Well, he sure helped get you off that cliff," said Tim O'Conner.

"I know, Dad," said Rufe. "Without Silver, TJ never could've gotten back so fast with that rope. I wouldn't have been able to hang on." Silver was basking in the attention and praise.

"Tim," said John Flint, "I understand you and the boys been fixing up your old service station."

"Yeah, John. You know, after Martha died and I started to drink, people got where they wouldn't trust me to fix their car... not that I blame 'em. Now that I quit drinking, I think I can get their business back again. If I can work on a few cars and tractors, do some welding and sell some gas, it should be enough to keep the wolf away from the door. Sorry, Silver," he said with a laugh. "*You're* welcome anytime!"

"No problem getting the business back, Tim," said Amos. "You always were the best mechanic around." John broke in:

"If you're working hard to get the garage back on track, Tim, you may not be able to help us with the tree harvest. We could use you and the boys for three days around December the tenth. I can't pay much, though."

"Don't you worry, John. We'll be here. As for pay, we don't need much. In fact, one of your trees will just about do it. Since Martha died, me and the boys ain't had much for Christmases. This year, we thought we'd try to do a nice tree and have a real Christmas. Ain't that right, Ned?"

"Right, Dad," Ned answered in a quiet voice. "It won't be like it was with Mom, but it'll be nice for us to have Christmas again."

"I can't let you work up here for nothing but a tree, Tim" said John Flint.

"You sure *can*, John," said Tim. "You and your family done some things for us that we can't never pay back, but I sure aim to try. Ain't no way you can stop me."

"OK, Tim, you don't have to feel that way, but, if you *do*, we sure will accept the help and be grateful for it. One condition, though: you and the boys come over for Christmas dinner, right Betsy?"

"I got a big enough turkey in that pen out there to feed ten people!" said Betsy.

Tim looked doubtful.

"Dad," said Ned, "*you* can't cook a turkey, say yes."

"He's right," said Tim with a grin. "It's a deal."

After they had finished off the beef stew

and the apple cobbler, they all pushed back from the table.

"Whew!" said Joe, "that apple cobbler 'bout finished me. Now that we're all full and happy, let's talk some more about this tree harvest."

"What about the weather, John?" asked Amos. "That worries me. Could snow stop us harvesting the trees?"

"Yeah, I worry too. We got a whole town depending on us for Christmas trees. But heck, Amos, my tractor can handle *a lot* of snow, and yours is even better. I plan to keep some tractor paths scraped out up through the fields. If I stay ahead of the snow, it'll take a blizzard to stop us. I got two chain saws and you got one. The first day, while you and me and Tim cut, Jane and Betsy and the kids can be dragging the trees to the tractor paths. Then the next day, Joe and Rocky can drive the tractors while you and me and Tim load the trailers. Betsy and Jane and the kids can stay down at the station and load the flatcars. The tractors can pull up right alongside of

'em so that part should work good. Ned and Rufe are gonna come in mighty handy. Also, if something breaks down, we got our own mechanic on the spot to fix it." He grinned at Tim.

"I'll bring my tools along, just in case," said Tim.

Amos broke in: "So you think we can do it in two days, John?"

"Yeah, but I'm gonna allow an extra day in case something goes wrong. The train comes through around five Thursday afternoon. That's the twelfth. If we start to harvest on Tuesday the tenth, we should have plenty of time."

"All right, enough business," said Rocky, getting out his guitar. "I'm gonna sing you folks some railroad songs whether you like it or not. If you don't like my singin', I sure hope you'll lie about it! One of these days I'm gonna write my own railroad song about one of the trains I worked on. I ain't done it yet, though, so how 'bout we start off with *The Wabash Cannonball*?"

84   John Flint threw another log on the fire

and shut off the lights. TJ stretched out on the floor to listen, with his head on Silver. He watched the firelight flicker on the walls and his head moved up and down with Silver's breathing. Soon they all joined in:

"Listen to the jingle, the rumble and the roar,

As she glides along the woodland,

Through the hills and by the shore..."

11

O N DECEMBER TENTH, HARVEST DAY, THE Flints were up at daybreak. There had been a dusting of snow but not enough to hinder the harvest. Joe and Rocky, the Fisks and the O'Conners all gathered in Betsy's kitchen where she fortified them with pancakes, maple syrup and coffee. They were in the fields by eight.

The harvest went even better than planned. There was a minor tractor breakdown which Tim fixed, but everything went smoothly. By the end of the day, not only were all of the trees cut, they had already taken ten trailer loads of trees to the station and loaded them on one of the flatcars. By the end of the second day there were three railroad cars stacked high with the Flint Christmas trees, and the trees were all tied down and secure. They were too tired to celebrate, but everyone agreed to meet at the station the following day to see the southbound freight pick up the trees.

That night, after letting the dogs out, the Flints sat down for a glass of milk and a sandwich.

"It went well, John," Betsy said. "Looks like our worries are over."

"Yeah, Bets, it's all up to the railroad now. We can relax."

Little did they know.

The next day the whole harvest crew was on the platform at the station waiting for the southbound freight. Excitement was high. Even Silver seemed to feel it as he caught the snowballs Sally and TJ threw. He looked confused as the snow powdered to nothing in his mouth. The twins were pushing and shoving each other, about to get in a fight from arguing over who had done the most work the day before, and Tim had to break it up. They heard a whistle in the distance.

"That's her," said Joe, "right on time, too."

The train approached the station at about forty miles an hour.

"She ain't slowing!" said Joe.

"She sure ain't!" said Rocky. "What's goin' on?"

As the train rocketed past the station, they realized there was a private car on the end of the train. They could see two men in the well-lighted car having drinks at a table. One of them was smoking a cigar.

"That was L.T. Broon's private car," said Joe. "That was him inside with the cigar. He owns the railroad. I've known him for years."

Mac McCorkle, the Station Master, came running out of his office waving a slip of paper.

"John, your pickup's been canceled," he said. "Mr. Broon's orders."

"I see that," John said dryly, shaking his head in disbelief.

"Your shipment's been rescheduled for the next freight."

"When's that?" asked John.

"The day after Christmas."

"Well *that's* something!" said John. "The railroad's gonna deliver our Christmas trees the day after Christmas! Mac, there are usually two freights a *week* through here."

"I know, John, but business has been bad, and they cut back even more on account of Christmas. There's passenger service every two days, but the next freight's on the twenty sixth. I'm gonna call Rutland and see if I can figure out what happened."

Betsy went up to Joe Tanner.

"Dad," she said, "what about two-forty-two?"

"I been standing here thinking the same thing, Honey, it might work."

"Two-forty what?" said John.

"Dad's old engine. Two-forty-two. It still runs. Maybe we can haul the trees into Twin Forks with two-forty-two."

"Is that possible, Joe" asked John.

"Well, yeah, it's possible. The old gal runs as good as ever. Trouble is I'd have to get permission. The tracks belong to the Rutland

Railroad."

"How could you do that?"

"I guess the simplest way would be to talk to Broon. Heck, I've known him for twenty years, ever since his daddy had him working as freight dispatcher down in Bennington. Let's go see if Mac can catch up with him in Rutland." They headed for the office just as Mac was coming out.

"Here's the story, John. Evidently the dispatcher told Mr. Broon that your shipment here was trees. Didn't say anything about Christmas. Mr. Broon must've thought it was trees for the lumber mill and figured a delay wouldn't matter. He needed to get to an important meeting in Rutland, so he had 'em hook up his private car and run straight through. That's what happened, near as I can figure out."

"Thanks, Mac," John said. Then he explained the plan about using two-forty-two. Mac agreed to try to reach Broon when the train reached Rutland, and they all went into the little waiting room. Mac lit up the little potbelly stove.

90

"Thanks, Mac," Betsy said. "At least we can be warm while we wait."

Two hours later the call came through from Broon. Betsy and John went into the little office and listened while Joe explained the problem.

"...I *know* it's irregular, L.T.," Joe was saying, "but having two thousand Christmas trees show up the day after Christmas is irregular *too*."

"...What do you mean it ain't legal? What ain't legal? I'm still a licensed engine driver, and you know it."

"...I hear you sayin' 'no', L.T., but you need to change your mind."

"...I *will* tell you why. How are you gonna look when it comes out that you caused a whole town to lose their Christmas trees, L.T.? Think about it. A *whole town* with no Christmas trees because L.T. Broon had to get

91

to his important meeting. People think Scrooge was mean, but you're fixin' to make Scrooge look downright friendly. Aside from you makin' yourself the most disliked man in Vermont, what good do you think it's gonna do your railroad to have this story getting about?" He paused for breath and, raising his eyebrows, looked at the others. The phone was silent. Evidently, L.T. Broon was thinking.

"...Yeah, I'm still here, L.T.," said Joe.

"...No, I ain't threatening you. I wouldn't spread the story, but the truth is bound to come out. Too many people already know what happened, and John here will have to tell the ministers down in Twin Forks why they didn't get their trees, and the ministers will have to tell everybody else." There was another long pause.

"...OK, L.T., I will. Yeah. Yes, I got a fireman, a real professional." He winked at Rocky who was standing in the doorway. "Right, L.T., here's Mac. Oh, L.T., ... *Thanks*! and... everybody here says, *merry Christmas*!" He put his hand over the mouthpiece before he handed the phone to Mac and turned to John and Betsy. "Thought he was gonna say '*bah humbug*'," he said with a grin, "but he said 'yes'!"

12

*T*HAT EVENING THEY ALL GATHERED AT THE
Flint house to make plans. Mac had found out
from the dispatcher that the tracks would be
free of traffic until the fourteenth.

Joe raised his hand to get everyone's attention.

"Listen, folks, we need to go tomorrow
afternoon and come back tomorrow night, so
we're off the tracks for the passenger train to
come through on the fourteenth. 'Course
tomorrow's Friday the thirteenth! Anybody
superstitious?"

"Heck no," said John.

"I am," said Amos, "but I'll ignore it."

"Good!" said Joe. "We'll just keep right on
makin' our own luck. Rocky and I can get up
steam by noon tomorrow. We'll be at the station by one. We'll hook up to the flatcars and
check everything over and plan to leave

around one-thirty. John, you can tell your ministers we'll be in Twin Forks about three-thirty. We'll come home tomorrow night. OK?"

"OK!" said John. "Now listen, everybody, all of you are invited along for the ride. I sure hope you'll come." A cheer went up.

"Wouldn't miss it!" said Tim.

"TJ and Sally can ride up in the cab with me and Rocky" said Joe. "Everybody else can ride in the caboose."

"Silver, too," said TJ.

"And Pip," said Sally.

"Why not," said John. "Ever had a squirrel for a passenger, Joe?"

"Nope, but with two thousand trees, we ought to have at least one squirrel!" Sally laughed with delight.

Jane said, "Betsy, you've been doing all the cooking lately. Tomorrow, I'll bring a big pot of my pea soup with ham in it and some of my sourdough bread. That'll stick to the ribs."

"*Wonderful*," said Betsy. "I *love* your split pea soup, Jane."

Rocky chimed in:

95

"We need a name for this train, an' I got an idea...what about...'The Christmas Tree Express'?"

"Great idea, Rocky!" said John.

"That gives *me* an idea," said Betsy. She left the room. When she came back, she had a bolt of red cloth and a can of green paint.

"What do you say we make a banner for the train," she said. "Who's good at painting letters?"

"Me," said Jane. "I used to do lots of posters in college. I'll take it home and do it tonight. How much of that fabric do you want me to use?"

"Use it all, Jane. I've had it for years. There's about fifteen feet there. If you cut it in half lengthways, and sew the two pieces together, we'll get a banner about thirty feet long. We can tie it on the middle flatcar." The phone rang, and John went into the hall to get it. When he came back, he said:

"That was Father Denis. They got really upset down in Twin Forks when the train came through and didn't even stop. I told him what happened. When I explained about The

Christmas Tree Express, he got really excited. I wouldn't be surprised if every kid in town didn't show up at the station tomorrow, some of the grownups, *too*."

"Gonna be hard to sleep tonight!" said TJ.

"Sure is!" said Sally.

"Sure is!" said Ned and Rufe together.

13

FRIDAY THE THIRTEENTH OF DECEMBER
dawned cold and clear. TJ was too excited to
eat much breakfast, but by eleven he was
ready for the sandwich and hot chocolate his
mom had fixed. After they all had a sandwich, they bundled up in their winter coats,
scarves, knitted caps and gloves, and all piled
into the old Ford pickup. Silver, whose coat
was designed for sleeping outside in zero
weather, was delighted to ride in the back.
When they got to the station, they could see
that the Fisks and the O'Conners were already
there. They all stood around on the platform
talking excitedly, their breaths making little
puffs of steam in the cold December air. Rufe
said:

"Durn! Suppose they can't get it running."

"Heck, Rufe, don't worry about *that*," TJ
responded. "Granddad and Rocky been run-

98

nin' locomotives all their lives."

"I hear a bell!" said Ned.

Sure enough, from way in the distance they could hear the ding, ding, ding of an engine bell. Then they heard the whistle.

"Too too too,

too too too,

too too toooo to toooo..."

"What's he blowin'?" said Amos.

Rocky's got the Christmas spirit!" said Sally. "He's blowing *Jingle Bells*!"

In the distance, where the rails disappeared into the woods, they could now see a puff of smoke pluming rhythmically above the cedar trees. It crept towards the edge of the woods, and they began to hear the chuff, chuff, chuff. As they watched, the little engine, her shining brass fittings twinkling in the sun...her smoke stack and valves puffing and steaming bravely... broke out of the woods pulling the little red caboose.

"There she is!" shouted TJ. Two-forty-two!

Silver began to bark and Pip ran to the top of Sally's knitted cap and began to chitter.

"She's *comin' in*!" shouted TJ as they all began to cheer.

Bell ringing, the little engine puffed into the station and stopped by the platform. Joe Tanner leaned out grinning.

"She runs like she never was retired!" he said.

Rocky climbed down, uncoupled the caboose and signaled Joe to pull up. Joe took the little engine ahead, and Mac came out to switch the tracks so the engine could back onto the siding and pick up the three flatcars. Joe then pulled the engine and flatcars ahead onto the main tracks and, after Mac had reversed the switch, he backed the train until Rocky could couple the last flatcar to the caboose. Jane and Amos tied the bright red banner onto the middle flatcar. The bright green letters proudly proclaimed: THE CHRISTMAS TREE EXPRESS. The little train was ready. Rocky and Joe walked around the train checking everything and then climbed back up into the engine cab to check all the gauges. Finally Joe leaned out of the cab and called:

"All aboard the Christmas Tree Express. All aboard!"

The little train steamed across the snowy countryside. TJ sat on the left side of the cab and Sally on the right. They took turns with the whistle cord, which was great fun because it let off such a blast that pulling it was a powerful feeling. They blew *Jingle Bells* and, children and their parents, hearing the unusual signal, tumbled from the farmhouses to wave at the little train and her crew. They were always treated to another chorus of *Jingle Bells* on the whistle or the bell.

Back at the caboose, Ned and Rufe stood outside on the platform waving until they got

too cold, then they went into the cozy interior to toast themselves by the little potbellied stove. While they were getting warm, Jane and Amos took a turn on the platform, then Betsy, John and Tim took a turn. Silver sat on the bench in the booth looking at the scenery with great interest and barking when the whistle blew. Pip, on the other hand, was asleep, curled up in some pine straw in the bottom of a little box that Sally had made for him. The sky had gone gray and soon the Christmas feeling was increased by large, feathery snowflakes which began to put a frosting on the train.

"Look at that," said Amos, as the train rounded the long curve into Twin Forks. "The whole town has turned out." Hundreds of people were yelling and waving as The Christmas Tree Express pulled into the station.

As two-forty-two chuffed toward the platform, bell ringing, Rocky threw one more shovelful of coal into the firebox, put his shovel aside and came over to TJ.

"Give 'em one last chorus of *Jingle Bells*,"

CHAPTER 13

he said with a grin.

    "Too, too, too

    too, too, too

    too, too, toooo to toooo..."

14

*T*HEY UNCOUPLED THE CABOOSE, BACKED the three flatcars onto the siding and left them where they would have been left if the regular freight had hauled them. Two-forty-two's job was done, and Joe pulled the engine back out on the main tracks, backed down and hooked up to the caboose. They were ready for the trip home.

Father Denis gave John a check from each of the churches and made a little speech thanking John for the trees and Joe Tanner for making the Christmas Tree Express possible. There was a good deal of back slapping, hand-shaking and Christmas cheer all around, but it was almost dark, and the crowd was starting to leave. The crew from Masonville headed for the little caboose where Jane had the ham and split pea soup steaming on top of the woodstove.

Ned and Rufe were going to ride in the cab with Joe and Rocky on the return trip. Jane had insisted that the engine crew eat first. The four of them climbed into the booth and she served them steaming mugs filled with split pea soup and tender chunks of smoked ham with crunchy slices of buttered sourdough bread alongside.

"*Man*, that smells good," sighed Rocky, holding his face in the steam and inhaling deeply. "Is there enough for two mugs?"

"All you can eat," said Jane, smiling with pleasure.

The door of the caboose opened and John came in pulling off his coat and gloves.

"Yahoo!" he yelled, "We did it!" He grabbed Betsy, and hugged her so her feet came off the ground. "We're still in business, Bets! Now, let's go home." He put her down and went over to the booth.

"How do we turn this train around?" he asked Joe. "Do we have to *back* all the way home?"

"There's a big loop of tracks that goes over to the sawmill," Joe said. "It circles the town

107

and comes back into the main line about five miles north of here. We turn around by goin' that way. The stationmaster has already switched the tracks for us."

"Joe, you're a genius," said John. "Now I see where Betsy got her brains."

"'Bout time somebody recognized it!" said Joe.

"Heck, no wonder I can't beat him at checkers," said Rocky.

After the excitement of the day, it was very peaceful riding along through the night in the little caboose. The wheels made a rhythmic, double click-clack on the rails, the wood stove kept them all cozy, and the brass oil lamp swung gently, causing shadows to dance on the walls.

Amos and Tim were in the booth finishing off a third mug of soup. Betsy was sitting on the bunk where John was stretched out. He

was resting his head on her lap and she stroked his brow, soothing away the tensions caused by the last few days. Jane, who had brought her guitar along, was sitting on the forward bunk, her legs hanging over the edge, quietly strumming chords, and TJ, Silver and Sally were on the third bunk with Pip who was asleep again curled up in Sally's knitted cap as if it were a nest.

"That squirrel sure can sleep," said TJ.

"It's hibernatin' time for him," said Sally. "TJ, what did you ask for for Christmas?"

"A BB gun and a scout camping knife," answered TJ.

"I'll be darned," said Sally, "I did *too*."

"No dollhouse for you, huh, Sally?"

"What in the world would I do with a doll-house?" said Sally.

"Yeah, see what you mean."

"TJ, let's do some camping next summer."

"Great idea, Sally. We could take Silver and camp at the beaver pond up on Bear Mountain."

Amos said,"Jane, sing us a Christmas carol."

110

"Yeah, Mom, but don't sing *Jingle Bells*," said Sally with a grin. "I'm tired of that one."

Betsy said,"Jane, sing us the carol about the first Christmas eve that your mother taught you when you were a girl."

As they rode together through the cold December night, warm in the little caboose, safe and secure as only families and close friends can be, Jane strummed a minor chord and sang:

THE FIRST CHRISTMAS EVE

Wanderers traveling through the night,
Seeking the comfort of shelter and light,
Would no inn or home receive
Wanderers on *The First Christmas Eve*

There was a light that appeared in the east,
As a sign to man and beast,
Would the eyes that saw believe
The star that shone down on *The First Christmas Eve?*

Wise men saw, and without questioning,
Followed the light from afar.
Shepherds in their awe and wonder,
Knelt in the light of the star.

Traveling still were the young man and
wife,
Carrying their sweet burden of life,
Who would their weary need relieve,
Sheltering them on *The First Christmas
Eve*

Then in a stable in Bethlehem,
A setting so plain for the perfect gem,
The maid lay down her weary head,
Straw from the manger she used for a bed.

There she rested through the night,
Waiting to bring the gift of light,
Waiting for the morrow's birth,
That would bring light to all the earth.

Every hope for every babe and
Each shining star we believe,
Every deed of love and comfort

Honors *The First Christmas Eve*.

As we go forward through the years,
Filled with hopes and dreams and fears,
Let's look back and all receive
Strength from remembering *The First Christmas Eve*.

15

*I*T WAS CHRISTMAS EVE AND, AT THE FLINT
house, TJ and his folks were admiring the
Christmas tree. The lamps were out, and only
the lights from the tree and the firelight lit up
the room. They had been listening to
Christmas carols on the radio, and Betsy, who
had been working on Christmas dinner all
afternoon, came over and sat down next to TJ,
leaned back, sighed and stretched.

"Isn't it a pretty tree?" she said.

"I saved us a nice one," said John, "and the
price was right."

"You know," said TJ, "I just been sitting
here thinking...we're so lucky...we're *so*
lucky..." Betsy put her arm around him.

"We are, Teej. We *sure* are."

Christmas morning.

TJ was outside popping icicles off the edge of the roof with his new Daisy BB gun. He thought he heard some dogs, took one last shot and turned around. Coming down the road was a team of six dogs pulling a sled with Amos Fisk driving and Jane and Sally aboard.

"Merry Christmas!" called Amos as he drove into the Flint yard. John and Betsy came out pulling on coats. John held the door for Silver, whose appearance caused considerable excitement among the huskies. With his usual dignity, Silver ignored them and finally, Amos got them quieted down.

"Merry Christmas, folks!" said John. "Time for the surprise. It's in the barn." Sally and TJ were comparing BB guns.

"What's in the barn, Dad?" said TJ.

"A joint present for you and Sally," said John. "Mom and I and the Fisks bought it for you two to use together. It's a surprise." He went into the barn and came out with something big that had an old quilt thrown over it. He put it down and pulled off the quilt. It was a beautifully varnished two-man dogsled with bright red trim.

"With all this snow we have," Amos said, "we thought you two ought to have a sled that had runners instead of wheels. Merry Christmas, kids!" Jane, Betsy and John chimed in: "Merry Christmas!"

"Wow!" said TJ.

"Wow!" said Sally.

Silver came up and, tail wagging like mad, started to whine and look up at TJ.

"I know what *he's* saying," said TJ.

"Yeah, *me too*," said Sally. "He's saying, '*Let's go*!'"

CHAPTER 15

T H E   E N D